Julie W___

CONTENTS

The publishers wish to acknowledge the assistance of Margaret Pattenden, M.S.T.A. and Daphne Wilkinson, M.S.T.A. (ex Olympic swimmer) for their assistance when planning this book.

How to
SWIM
and DIVE

by HENRY MARLOW

with illustrations by
MARTIN AITCHISON

Publishers: Ladybird Books Ltd . Loughborough
© Ladybird Books Ltd (formerly Wills & Hepworth Ltd) 1971
Printed in England

Why Swim?

Swimming is a pastime that can be enjoyed all the year round. It can be carried on out-of-doors in the sea, river or lido and indoors in heated pools all over the country. You can swim with your family or your friends, or on your own when you reach a sufficiently high standard. You need very little equipment and you can begin at an early age and continue for as many years as you feel inclined.

You may wish to swim simply for fun or regard swimming as a competitive sport. Either way, it is a healthy form of activity in which every part of the body is exercised. If you intend to take up other water sports such as sailing, water-skiing or surf-riding, it is absolutely essential that you first learn to swim so that, in an emergency, you can reach the shore or keep yourself afloat in the water until help arrives.

Finally, swimming offers a method by which the physically handicapped can strengthen weak limbs and exercise bodies which can hardly be moved at all without the extra support provided by the water.

A correct start to swimming brings confidence in the water.

0 7214 0285 2

Where to Swim

We are all made differently. Some of us take to the water like ducks while others need a lot of persuasion to get even their feet wet. Every year at the seaside you will see unwilling children being dragged screaming into the water by parents who think that tough measures are the best: other more fortunate youngsters are allowed to splash about contentedly at the water's edge.

Indeed, the wide expanse of sea can be quite frightening for the nervous beginner, who may be completely discouraged by a wave hitting his face causing him to swallow mouthfuls of salt water and leaving him gasping for air.

By far the best place to learn the art of swimming is in a public bath and it does not matter whether this is in the open air or indoors. Here you can learn to swim under controlled conditions. The shallow and deep ends are clearly indicated and the various depths of water are marked along the sides. There are no awkward waves to worry you and the pool, being enclosed, always gives you an aiming point at the other side of the water.

Getting into the Water

The first thing you have to do is to get into the water, and each time you visit the baths it is a good idea to try a different method. No doubt you will begin by creeping cautiously backward down the steps at the shallow end (1)—quite right too. But do not be satisfied with this method of entry more than once or twice. Next, try lowering yourself into the water from the side, supporting your body with your arms and going in backwards (2). After this, try a little forward jump with your feet on the edge of the scum trough or rail (3). Keep your shoulders well forward, hips and knees bent. The water is shallow so you will want your knees bent when your feet land on the bottom.

Next try jumping in from the top step (4) and then from the side of the bath. At this stage you will feel your confidence growing and you can try a short, running jump (5), but do make sure no other bather is in the way.

Once in the water, you will discover that you cannot move as easily as you can on dry land. Never try to run but always walk by sliding your feet along the bottom.

Remember—the shallow end is your end until you can swim.

Getting used to the Water

If, in the early stages, you are nervous of the water there is no need to worry. This is a normal feeling toward something you know very little about, and it takes a little while to get used to moving about in water. Do not be in too much of a hurry but take each process stage by stage and you will soon find yourself enjoying your new experience.

Most beginners do everything possible to avoid putting their faces in the water, yet this is something that must be done before you can learn to swim properly. So, stand in the shallow end of the pool, bend your knees until your shoulders are under the water and your chin just on the surface (1). Hold your breath, shut your eyes and duck your face under the water for a second or two (2). You may not enjoy the experience but when you have recovered do it again. In time you will be able to stay in this position for many seconds and feel quite relaxed.

Later you can try keeping your eyes open under the water and looking at your feet. All swimming should be done with eyes open.

1

2

Learning to Breathe

We must all breathe to live and under normal circumstances we do it unconsciously, only noticing any effort when we take some strenuous exercise. When we stand in water up to our neck, the pressure of the water against our body makes breathing a little more difficult. However, the body soon adapts itself and the effect will not last for long.

The main thing to remember is that breathing-in can only be done when the mouth is out of the water; when it is under the surface the breath must be held or expelled. There is no need to take in a great lungful of air before going under. This will merely give you a 'bursting' sensation after a few seconds. A normal breath is quite enough and far more comfortable.

A swimmer must, of course, breathe out as well as in and not simply hold his breath under water. And so we must next learn a breathing rhythm in which the air breathed *in* with the mouth just out of the water (1) is breathed *out* when the face is in the water (2). This rhythm will take time to develop and you can practise it after the exercise described on the previous page.

When you see a first-class swimmer, notice the rhythm of his breathing.

How we can Float in Water

Everything has a certain *density* and the density of an object compared with the density of water is known as its *specific gravity*. Water, being the standard, is given a specific gravity figure of 1.00. Thus, if an object has a specific gravity of less than 1.00 it will float, if it is more than 1.00 it will sink.

The average human body containing a normal amount of air has a specific gravity of 0.98. This means it will just float, with 98 per cent below the surface and the remaining 2 per cent above. So long as we have the usual amount of air in our body we can stay afloat but if we breathe out too much our specific gravity will rise and we will sink.

In addition to its specific gravity, an object in water has two forces acting vertically upon it; its weight acting downward through the force of gravity, and the *buoyancy* of the water which acts in an upward direction. The object will float if the two forces are equal. Our feeling of 'weightlessness' in water is due to the force of buoyancy holding us up.

The air contained in the body and the ball makes the difference between floating and sinking.

Floating Exercises

It is one thing being told you can float but quite another to prove it for yourself, and there are some exercises designed to help you. If you have overcome the submerging and underwater breathing problems these exercises will be quite easy. Furthermore, they will help you to gain even greater confidence in the water.

First relax. Hold your arms out in front of you, palms of hands downward (1). Keeping your legs straight, lean forward until your face is in the water (2). You will now be lying in the water, your weight supported by its buoyancy. When you have had enough you can stand up again by pushing downward with your hands, lifting your head and bringing your knees forward.

Next, you may like to try *mushroom floating*. Stand in the crouch position with knees bent, shoulders under the surface and chin just above (3). Lean forward, tucking your head down as you go. Your feet will rise off the bottom. Bring your knees up and grasp them with your hands. You will now be floating in the water with only your curved back showing above the surface like a mushroom (4). You can stand up again as before.

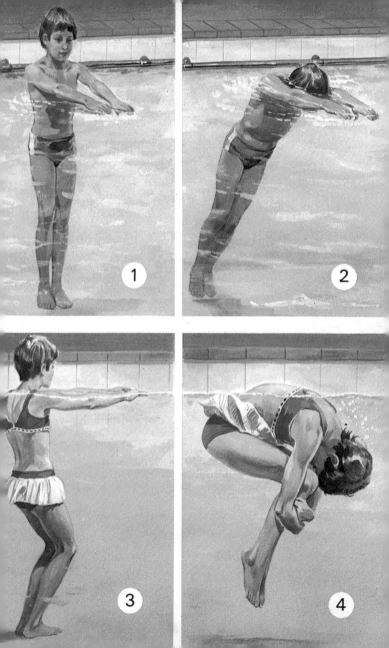

Gliding

Continue practising the floating exercises until you can do them in a relaxed manner. By this time you will have complete confidence in the water's ability to hold you up and you should have no difficulty in gliding.

Stand up straight and raise your hands above your head. Take a normal breath and hold it (1). Bend your knees until your head is under water, lean your body forward and push off with your feet against the bottom of the bath (2). You are now gliding (3).

Gliding can also be done from the side of the bath (4). Take up the starting position of the mushroom float, facing away from the side and as close to it as possible; pulling up your feet and dropping your head come more or less as one movement. When you feel your feet against the tiles, extend your arms forward, palms of hands down, and straighten your legs (5). You will find yourself gliding quite quickly through the water. Repeat this exercise several times trying to glide a greater distance each time.

Now try gliding to the bottom. Start off from the mushroom float (6) but instead of gliding forward, tuck your head down and see if you can touch the bottom with your hands (7). Stand up in the usual way.

Gliding on your Back

Gliding face downward, or prone, gives you the basic body position for the forward swimming strokes, but before you go on to these you should practise gliding on your back, which is the basic position for the back strokes. Actually, many beginners find the back stroke the easiest to learn.

Face the side of the bath and take hold of the trough or rail with both hands. Bring the feet up from the bottom and press them against the side a few inches below the hands (1). The water supports most of your weight in this position and you will have no difficulty in holding it. Release your grip on the trough and push quietly away from the side by straightening your legs (2). If you keep your head well back, ears under the water, you should be able to glide smoothly in the horizontal position with your arms at your sides (3).

When you wish to stand up again, swing your arms outward under the surface until they are in line with your shoulders. Push downward with the palms of the hands, at the same time lifting the head and bending the knees.

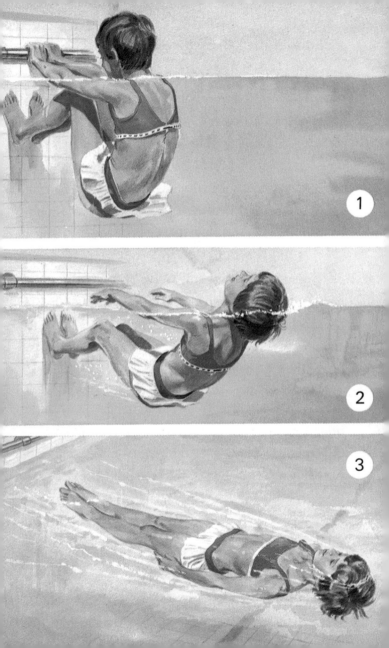

Hand and Arm Propulsion

Take up the crouch position; knees bent and chin at water level (1). Reach forward with your arms, placing the hands, palms downward, an inch or two below the surface (2). Keeping your body in the same position, press downward with the hands until they reach your sides. As you go through the movement you will find that your feet rise off the bottom (3). Repeat the action until you can do it easily. Now do the same arm movement again (4 and 5) but this time push your hands backward past your sides (6). Not only will your feet rise but your body will move forward through the water as well. Go back to the crouch position by moving the hands forward and upward through the water. You can paddle yourself across the bath by this method.

Next, try an arm *recovery* movement. Instead of bringing the arms forward through the water after the downward and backward push (7), complete the circle by swinging them out of the water (8) back to their forward position (9). As your hands re-enter the water in front of you, try not to splash. Practise the movement, leaning further forward with your face in the water.

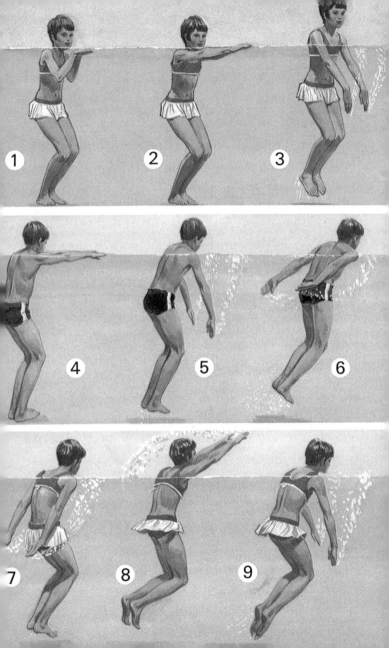

The Swimming Strokes

In this book for beginners, space does not allow us to describe the detailed movements of every stroke used in swimming. So we must concentrate on the basic actions of the more popular and useful strokes. The information will take you a long way in your enjoyment of the pastime: refinements, turns and lesser-used strokes such as the *Butterfly* can be added later.

The main strokes are as follows:

1. *Front Crawl*. This is the fastest stroke; used generally both for short sprints as well as long-distance events like swimming the Channel.

2. *Back Crawl*. Similar action to the front crawl but swum on the back. Often the first stroke to be learned as there are fewer problems to overcome in mastering the correct breathing.

3. *Breast Stroke*. A very pleasant, all-purpose stroke; probably the oldest method of swimming. Also used for underwater swimming, as all the movements are made under the surface.

4. *English Back Stroke*. Not included in competitive swimming but an easy stroke to perform. Also used in life-saving with a slightly modified leg kick.

ENGLISH BACK STROKE

ONT CRAWL

EAST STROKE

BACK CRAWL

BUTTERFLY

Butterfly stroke is not dealt with in this book

Front Crawl—Leg Action

We do something like the leg action of the crawl many thousands of times a day when we walk about. Of course, we do this in the upright position whereas we are horizontal when swimming, but the general movements are very similar. The most important thing to remember is that, for the crawl, you do not kick the legs from the knees but swing them up and down from the hips. The swing should be a shallow one, not more than eighteen inches deep at the bottom of the stroke and the feet should remain an inch or two below the surface at the top of the stroke, with the soles facing upward. The legs and ankles are kept generally straight but flexible because the knees will naturally bend slightly at the beginning of the down movement (1) and (2).

You can practise the leg action in the forward gliding position, swinging your legs up and down after pushing off from the side. Move them slowly at first and try not to make any splash. When you need to breathe, blow the air out of your mouth under water (3) and lift your face to take a fresh breath (4).

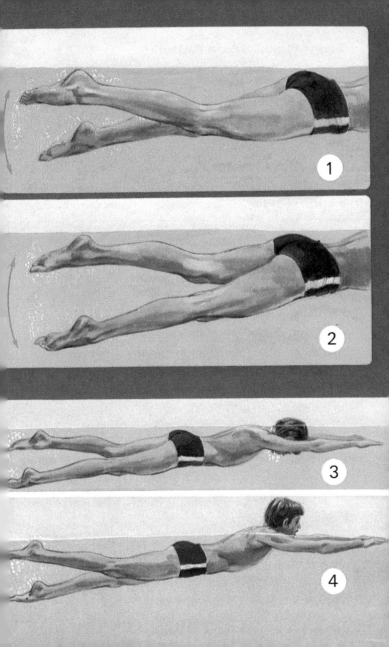

Front Crawl—Arm Action

Although we can propel ourselves along as described on the previous page, in the complete crawl stroke the legs act more as stabilisers and assist buoyancy while the main drive comes from the arms.

The arms work alternately. While one is under the water propelling you forward, the other is recovering out of the water. Let us see what happens. The hand enters the water ahead of and in line with the shoulder, fingers leading and wrist relaxed. The arm is slightly bent, with the elbow higher than the shoulder (1). You then force your hand forward and downward. As your hand gets a grip on the water, it starts to pull you forward (2). The movement is continued in a backward direction and from a point below the shoulder the pull turns into a push (3). When the elbow breaks the surface at the end of the stroke, the hand must be carried forward out of the water on the recovery (4). The process is then repeated.

Arm action can be practised in the crouch position which you adopted for earlier exercises (5). Go through the movements with one arm at a time before trying both in sequence—one arm recovering while the other is propelling.

The last picture shows a first-class swimmer from beneath the surface. Notice how the hand passes directly under the body.

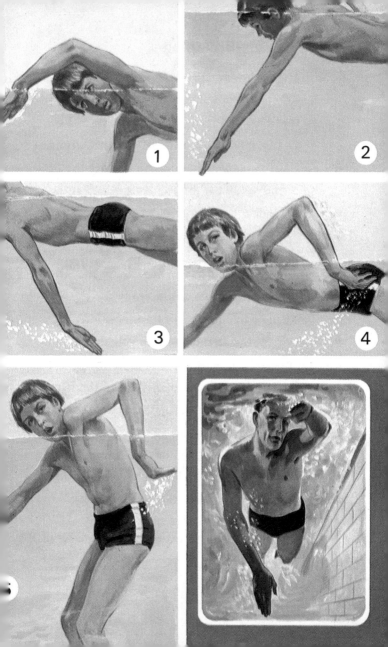

Front Crawl—Breathing

When you have practised the leg and arm actions of the crawl separately, you can try putting the two movements together and really start swimming. You now come to the most difficult part of the stroke, i.e., breathing. This is usually done by turning the head to one side, and you must first discover which is the most convenient side for you.

We will assume that you decide to turn your head to the left. When the left hand enters the water, the right arm will be about to come out ready for the recovery and you will be in a face-downward position (1). As the left arm drives through the stroke you should blow air out through your mouth (2). The right arm now comes forward, starts its downward stroke and the left elbow breaks surface. *Now* turn your head to the left, and breathe in during the left arm recovery (3). Before the end of this movement you should have taken your breath and by the time the left hand re-enters the water your face will again be looking downward (4).

Start by practising arm action and breathing in the crouch position.

Back Crawl

The leg action of the back crawl is very similar to that of the front crawl except, of course, it is performed on the back. The legs swing up and down from the hips and should remain relaxed and flexible to allow for natural bending. The feet should not break surface and splash, and the depth of swing should be about twelve inches or slightly less. You can practise the leg action in the back gliding position with your arms at your sides.

As with the crawl, the arms work alternately and do most of the propulsion. The hand enters the water ahead of the shoulder, edge of palm first (1), and in as straight a line with the shoulder as you can reasonably manage. Some swimmers, especially older ones, may have stiff shoulders and will have to be satisfied with a fairly wide entry point. The hand is forced sideways (2) and downward and continues through the stroke, first pulling then pushing, until the elbow touches the body (3). It is then taken out of the water and recovered at a low angle above the surface (4). This action is repeated with each arm in turn.

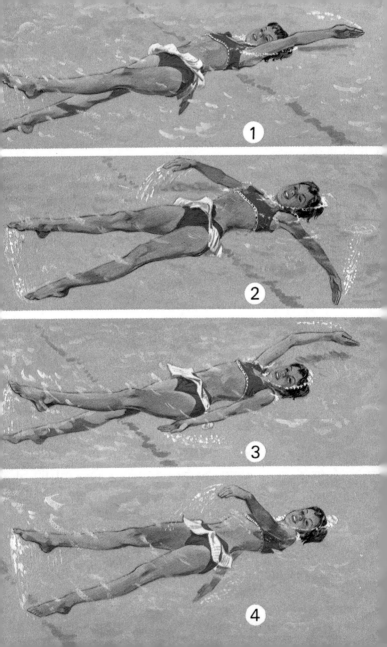

Breast Stroke—Leg Action

The breast stroke starts from the forward gliding position with the arms stretched forward in front of the head, hands fairly close together a few inches below the surface, palms facing downward. The legs are together and straight, and the toes are pointed backward. The head should be in a comfortable position with the chin just about at water level.

In contrast to the front and back crawls, the legs provide most of the forward drive. From the glide position (1) we start with the leg recovery. The heels are drawn upward toward the body and at the same time, the knees open outward (2). At the end of this rather frog-like movement the heels should be about twelve inches apart and the toes pointing outward (3). The feet are now kicked firmly sideways and backward in a circular motion, the soles of the feet facing the direction of the kick (4). This backward kick provides the forward drive for the body and the more vigorously it is performed the greater will be the body's forward thrust through the water.

At the completion of the kick the legs will be straight and together, back in the glide position. The recovery and kick are then repeated.

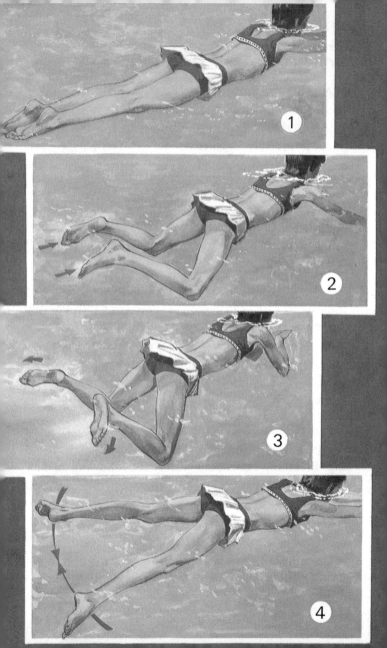

Breast Stroke—
Arm Action, Timing and Breathing

Arm action starts from the fully-extended position (1). It consists of a sideways and downward pull (2), with the palms of the hands turned outward to give the greatest possible pressure against the water. The hands travel eighteen or more inches below the surface and the propelling movement is completed when they are about level with and below the shoulders. The elbows must now be bent and the hands brought together just forward of the head, ready to be gently extended again in the recovery (3).

The timing of arm and leg actions is obviously important. From the gliding position the hands begin to pull sideways and downward while the legs are extended. As the arms near the end of their pulling stroke, the knees bend and the heels are brought forward. The kick is now made while the arms are being extended in recovery.

Breathing-in occurs naturally when the arms are completing their pulling stroke and the legs are recovering. Breathing-out is done during the following leg kick and arm recovery. As in all swimming, this breathing rhythm is most important; indeed, it is really part of the stroke.

The diagrams show the action of arms and legs together. (Follow the arrow for sequence.)

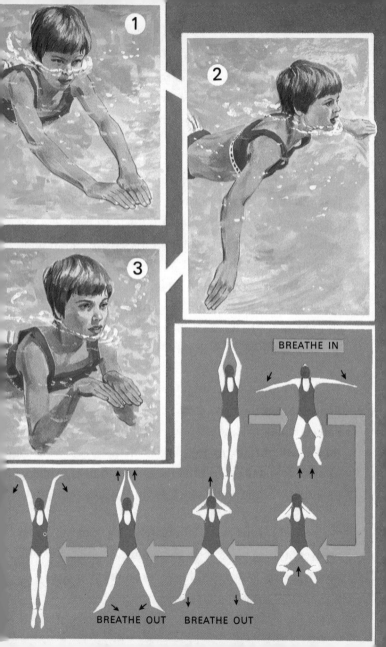

BREATHE IN

BREATHE OUT BREATHE OUT

English Back Stroke

This is one of the older strokes and not included in competitive events. However, it is a pleasant alternative to the back crawl and forms the basis of the life-saving stroke.

It starts from the back glide position, head slightly raised and arms at the sides (1). From this position, lower the feet by bending the knees until the lower legs are almost at right angles to the body. At the same time, open out the knees until they are some twenty to twenty-four inches apart, keeping the heels together (2). Now kick outward and upward with the feet (3), straightening the knees and bringing the feet together again into the glide position (4).

The arm movement begins with both arms extended in advance of the head, back of hands together. Pull the hands downward and sideways (5), fingers leading, until they reach the thighs (6). The arms are recovered by moving the hands in front of the body and then swinging them clear of the water, back to the extended position.

Legs and arms work alternately, leg kick and arm recovery taking place at the same time. Breathe in during arm recovery and out while the arms are pulling.

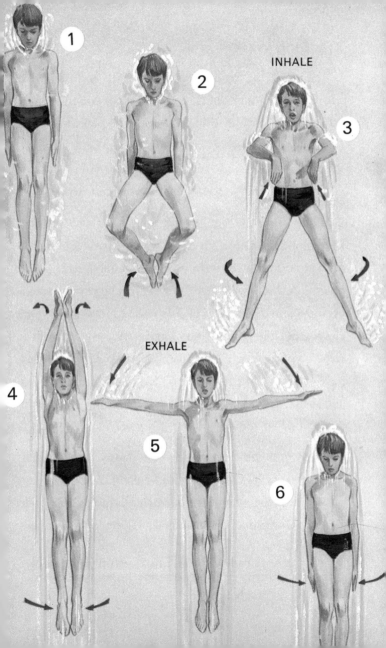

INHALE

EXHALE

Treading Water

The ability to tread water is a useful one in any sort of emergency when it may be necessary for you to support yourself in the water while waiting to be picked up. It is a method of staying afloat in the upright position keeping your head above the surface. Do not try it until you are confident in swimming out of your depth.

With your body upright, tilt your head backward to keep mouth and nose out of the water. Move your hands inward and outward in front of you, angled so that the palms press sideways and downward against the water as they move easily to and fro. Keep the wrists and elbows flexible. While your hands are moving as described, your legs will be performing the breast stroke leg kick in the vertical position. Do both arm and leg actions (1, 2, 3, 4) in a gentle, relaxed manner to avoid tiring yourself too quickly.

When you can tread water confidently, try doing it with hands or legs only, or with one hand or one leg out of action. Try it again with one or both hands held high above your head as if you were signalling for assistance.

Arms and legs may work in any rhythm you prefer, not necessarily in the sequence illustrated here.

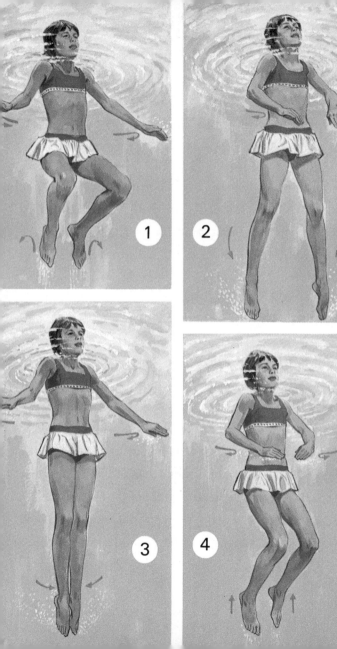

Learning to Dive

Diving is actually a sport in itself and a highly specialised one. However, we are more concerned here with diving simply as a means of entering the water or to enable you to start swimming.

Your first attempts can be made standing in the water at the shallow end of the bath. Raise both hands above your head and bend forward a little from the waist (1). Bend your knees (2) and leap upward (3), at the same time bending your body (4) at the hips and tucking your head well down (5). Practise this until you can stand vertically with your hands on the bottom (6).

Next, try a sitting dive from the side of the bath. Put your feet on the side rail or trough, stretch your arms out in front of you, fingers pointing toward the water (7). Look at the bottom of the bath and topple forward into the water, pushing off with your feet as you go (8). Try to enter the water at an angle of about forty-five degrees, keeping your arms and fingers outstretched in front of your head and your body and legs in a straight line. Your feet should be together and your toes pointed backward (9).

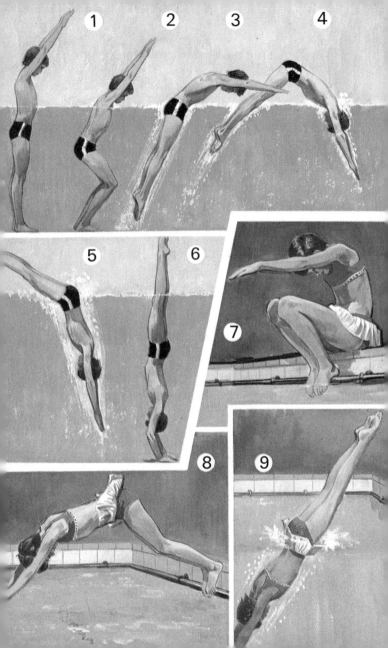

The Crouch and Standing Dives

When you can perform the sitting dive really well, go on to the crouch dive. But first make sure that the water is deep enough. It should never be less than five feet deep for the crouch and standing dives.

Stand in a crouching position with knees and hips bent and your toes gripping the edge of the bath. Extend your arms above your head and look at the water (1). Now straighten your knees and drive upward with your feet (2). If you keep your hips bent and your head tucked well down (3) you should be able to enter the water at a fairly steep angle. Straighten your hips as you go under (4). Practise the crouch dive until you can perform it easily and confidently.

You can now do a standing dive. Take up the same position at the side of the bath but this time have your knees and hips only slightly bent (5). Drive upward with knees and feet, keeping your hips bent and head down (6). You should enter the water vertically with your body, from fingers to toes, in a straight line and your hands and feet together (7).

When you have reached the required depth, turn your hands upward (8) to return to the surface.

The Plunge Dive

In contrast to the standing dive which has no real connection with swimming but is performed for fun, the plunge dive gets you into the water in a position from which the forward swimming strokes can be started. This is a very shallow dive, the body entering the water almost horizontally but with the head just a little lower than the feet.

Take up a relaxed crouch position, body bending well forward, feet about nine inches apart and toes gripping the edge of the bath. Allow your arms to hang loosely down from the shoulders, hands a little wider than the width of the body (1). Swing your arms backward then forward (2), straighten your knees and propel yourself off the side with your feet. Keep your head down and reach right forward with your hands, keeping them together in front of your head (3). Remain in the glide position until your body floats to the surface (4). Practise the plunge and glide until you can reach the other side of the bath without swimming a stroke.

Once you have mastered this dive, you can easily commence swimming the crawl or breast stroke as soon as your body rises to the surface.

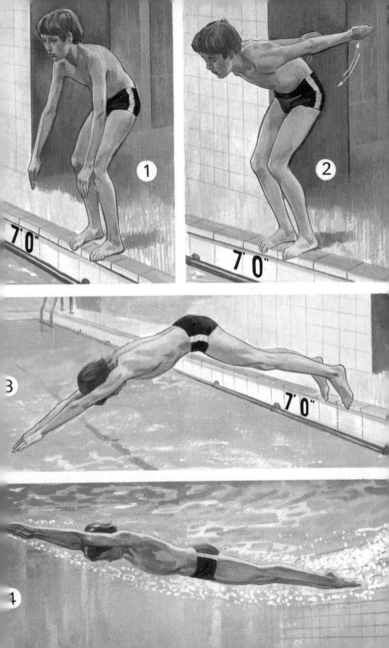

Life-saving Leg Kick

The life-saving leg kick is very similar to the leg kick of the English back stroke, but because the arms are used to support the victim's head or shoulders, the legs have to do all the work. Also, a drowning person's legs are inclined to sink and so prevent you from bringing your own feet together near the surface. Thus, instead of alternately kicking and recovering the legs, the feet should be moved in a continuous, circular motion. They should move outward, upward, inward and downward, pressure being applied to the water by the inside surfaces of the feet, legs and thighs. When you practise this kick, keep your hands on your chest or behind your head out of the way.

You can practise life-saving with a friend, holding him by the head, your palms covering his ears and your fingers on his forehead. His head should be resting on your chest as you perform the leg action (1). Another hold is under your friend's arms with his back on your chest (2).

Life-saving in all its aspects is a very specialised operation requiring expert instruction, but this brief introduction will give you a general idea.

Aids to Learning and Individual Styles

During the course of this book no mention has been made about artificial aids to swimming, such as water wings and inflatable rings and floats. Opinions differ greatly on this subject. Some experts consider that the use of these aids will help the learner to practise his strokes without having to worry about keeping himself afloat. Others believe that the sooner a beginner gets accustomed to and confidence in his own ability to float, the quicker he will learn to swim correctly. It has been said before that we are all made differently, and the author believes that it is up to each person to do whatever suits him, or her, best. Thus, all the leg and arm actions described in earlier pages may be practised with the use of artificial aids if you so wish.

Short or tubby people will not be able to perform all the swimming strokes in exactly the same way as people with slim, athletic figures. When you have learnt the correct actions, adapt them to suit your own particular build and style. One of the most important things in swimming is to be comfortable and relaxed in the water.

Of all the various swimming aids for the learner, the best is a professional instructor.

A Ladybird Book
Series 633